For Mom and Dad, who guide me when I'm lost.
And for Huey, a marvelous dog. —K.H.

For Jane and Aristides, whose dinner table
is famous for bringing people together —C.L.

Text copyright © 2020 by Kate Hoefler · Illustrations copyright © 2020 by Corinna Luyken

hmhbooks.com

The illustrations in this book were done in gouache, pencil, and ink on printmaking paper.
The text type was set in Stempel Garamond.
Book design by Jessica Handelman

Library of Congress Control Number: 2019039909

ISBN: 978-0-544-77478-0

Manufactured in China
SCP 10 9 8 7 6 5 4 3 2 1
4500799372

With gratitude to Kate O'Sullivan, Jessica Handelman,
and Steven Malk for holding the ropes with us.
—K.H. and C.L.

nothing
in
common

words by KATE HOEFLER

pictures by CORINNA LUYKEN

Houghton Mifflin Harcourt
Boston · New York

They had nothing in common,

so they never waved.

Except every day, they
loved watching the old
man with his dog.

The dog could do
marvelous things. And did.

Things they felt under the
floors of their hearts.

But other than that,
　　they had nothing in common.

Still, they were the only ones who
noticed when one day was different.

Neither had ever seen
an old man cry.

Or heard a name called
so sadly it flies through
your window and lands
on your chest.

It happened just to them.

When morning came, they both went out
with binoculars and a helmet for thinking.

Because a marvelous dog could be anywhere—
doing anything.

And a marvelous friend is hard to find.

They both knew that.

They looked on the same quiet rooftops,

and under the same whale,

and near the same planets.

And they thought of the same old man crying—
but other than that, they had nothing in common.

That day when a hot air balloon floated over the city, they were the only ones who thought a dog might be flying it—a marvelous dog who was lost and looking for his friend far and wide.

It could happen—

only they knew that.

It was a big way for a dog to look for someone.

And a big thing for just the two of them to notice.

But dogs aren't birds.

They can't see their way home from the sky.

Especially a dog without binoculars.

And a balloon is a
great moon with ropes.

You need another
person with a helmet.

Someone who knows exactly
where a balloon-dog wants to go.

Someone marvelous like that.

It was a slow walk—one with time to notice things.
Things they hadn't noticed before:

Tall things.

How patient a dog in the sky is.

How they both had the same feeling inside—
a deep feeling that ballooned out.

They pulled and pulled,
and they knew the same way back

because they knew the same stars.

And the same earth.

And the same quiet rooftops they saw
every night from their windows.

And because they'd noticed the same
old man every day, just the two of them.

An old man who cried—
this time, because he was happy.

Because the dog could do marvelous things.

And did.

Each thought the other was marvelous too—
even though they'd had nothing in common.

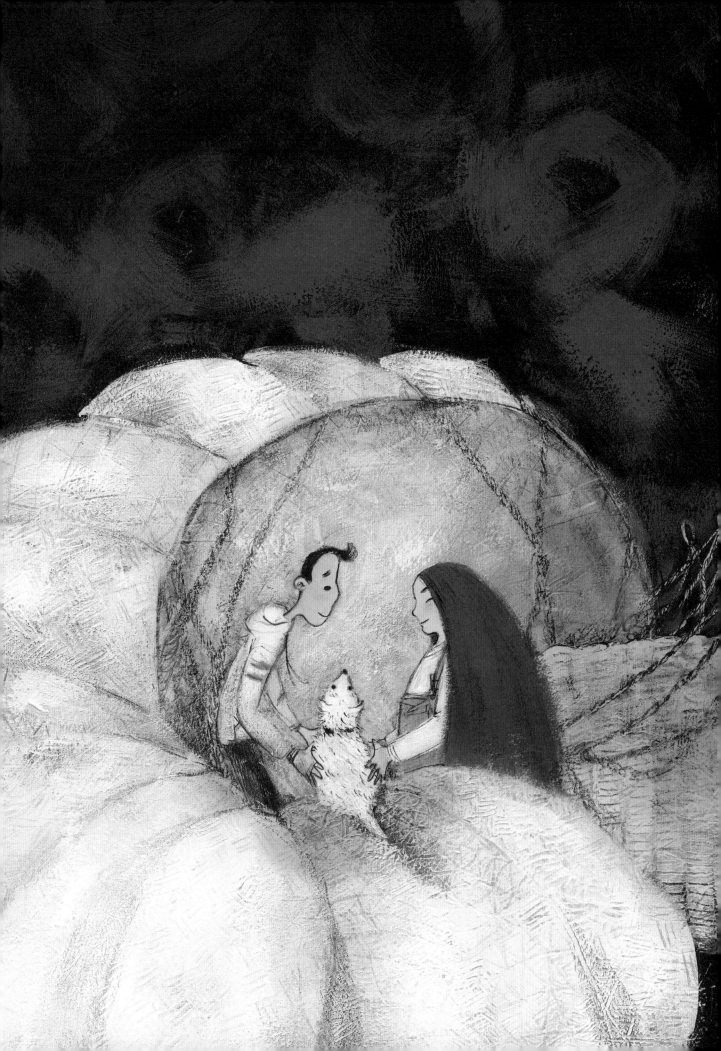

Nothing.

And that's something.